PRESENTED TO

Joe Mark, Bella, Juliana & Theodore

BY

Grandmama

ON

Dec. 25, 2014

John 3:16

ZONDERKIDZ

101 Bible Stories from Creation to Revelation
Copyright © 2013 by Zondervan
Illustrations © 2013 by Dan Andreasen

Requests for information should be addressed to:

Zonderkidz, 5300 Patterson Ave SE, Grand Rapids, Michigan 49530

ISBN 978-0-310-74064-3

Editor: Mary Hassinger
Art direction & design: Jody Langley

Printed in China

13 14 15 16 17 /DSC/ 6 5 4 3 2 1

101 Bible Stories

FROM CREATION TO REVELATION

Illustrated by
DAN ANDREASEN

TABLE OF CONTENTS

OLD TESTAMENT

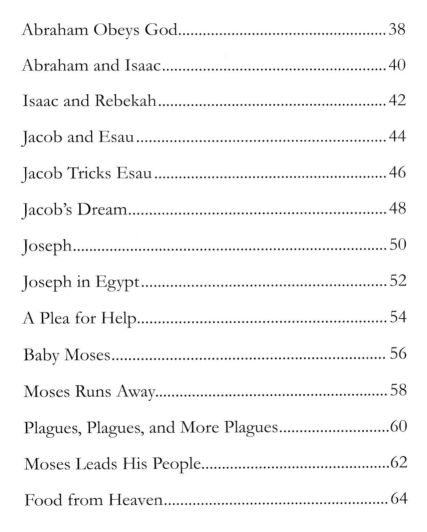

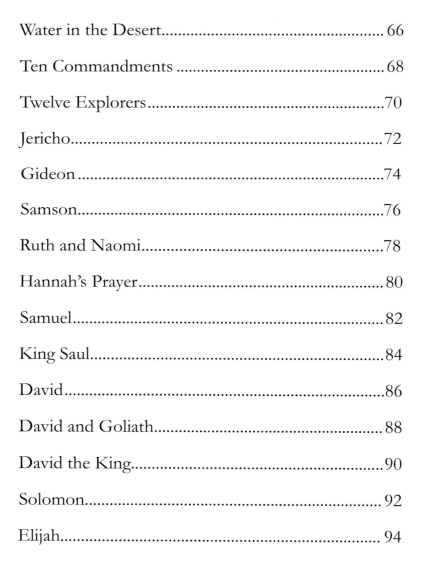

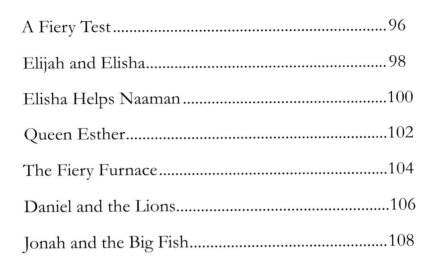

NEW TESTAMENT

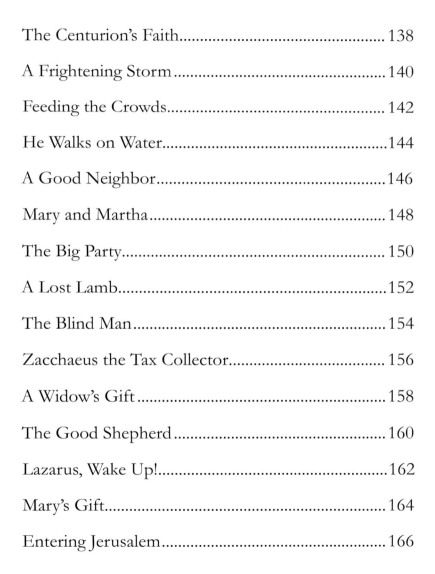

Old Testament

LET THERE BE LIGHT

Genesis 1:1–5

Long, long ago, God created the heavens and the earth. But the earth was blacker than black with darkness. And there was nothing but emptiness. Back then, the earth was a lonely place.

Then God said, "Let there be light!"

And there was light! God was pleased with the light, for it lit up the whole earth with its sunny brightness and golden warmth.

Now God knew this light was very good, but he did not stop there.

God gently made the earth to spin so that there could also be darkness. He called the dark "night," and the light he called "day."

THE SKY AND THE SEA

Genesis 1:6–10

God looked upon earth and said, "Now, let there be sky."

He spun layer upon layer of fresh, clean air around the earth, wrapping it in every shade of blue. And he continued until the sky was just right.

Then God poured out waters all over the earth. He made them flow pure and clean and clear.

Then God divided this gigantic body of water by forming huge mountains and wide valleys, rolling hills, and smooth, flat plains.

The water gathered into sparkling pools and deep blue lakes. And before long, fast-flowing rivers and bubbling streams rushed across the land to greet the mighty oceans.

17

And things began to grow

Genesis 1:11–13

God made the earth's soil rich and good. "Let the land produce!" commanded God.

Plants of all kinds began to spring forth from the soil. Tender shoots sprouted up from the ground to form fruit trees. Fragile green vegetable seedlings emerged, and soon tightly closed flower buds and blossoms appeared.

Soon the fruit trees grew big and strong. Their roots dug deep into the soil, and their branches hung heavy with sweet-smelling fruit. Tall, majestic evergreens stretched toward the sky, reaching their limbs up to heaven.

Luscious green grasses grew, and fragrant flowers bloomed in every color. And their precious seeds were caught by the winds and scattered far and wide. God painted the earth in breathtaking and colorful beauty. And it was so good!

CREATURES OF THE DEEP

Genesis 1:20–23

God looked upon the sleeping seas and created new life to grow there. He made tiny sea creatures and funny squids. He made gigantic whales and he even created powerful sharks! And to all these creatures God said, "Now grow and multiply and fill the sea."

Then God filled the fresh waters—the rivers and streams and lakes. He made sleek, silvery fish to swim through the rapids and bug-eyed frogs with strange, crooked legs. He made turtles with big, hard shells, and funny-looking crawdads with claws to pinch.

WINGS TO FLY

Genesis 1:20–23

"Let birds fill the skies," said God. And it was done.

Bright-colored birds, in all sizes and shapes, swept across the sky. God made beautiful swans, tiny hummingbirds, and soaring eagles. Soon the birds' twitters and chirps and peeps filled the land with happy music. And each day they lifted their voices in joyful praise.

HERE COME THE ANIMALS!

Genesis 1:24–25

The earth was a wonderful place, a beautiful place, but God had even more ideas.

So he created all kinds of animals. He made sleek gazelles, and elephants with floppy ears. He created the zebras and tigers with stripes; and to the giraffes and leopards, he gave lots of spots.

In other parts of the earth, God made different kinds of animals. In the icy cold regions, he made polar bears with warm, fuzzy coats, and black-and-white penguins that could slide in the snow.

In the cool forests of the north, God made graceful deer and majestic elk. He made bears and cougars. He made ring-tailed raccoons and rabbits, frisky squirrels and porcupines.

In the dry deserts, God made animals that could survive in the sun's bright heat and go without water for long periods of time.

God also made some very special animals that were not wild at all. He made horses and cows, dogs and cats, pigs and goats.

GOD MAKES MAN

Genesis 2:7–27

God was very pleased with all that he had made, and it was good. But still it was not enough. God wanted to create someone like himself. Someone who could be a friend.

So God scooped up a handful of dust from the earth. Then he gently blew his life into it. And God made man. God named this man Adam and set him in a very special garden called Eden.

God asked Adam to care for the plants and the animals and to give them names. He told Adam that all of Eden was for him to enjoy except for one thing. God told Adam not to eat from the tree in the center of the garden, because if he did, he would die.

Adam did just as God said, but he had no one to help him. And after a while, Adam became very lonely. The animals had each other, but Adam had no one that was like him.

God makes woman

Genesis 2:18–24

God did not want Adam to be lonely, so he made him fall asleep. While Adam slept, God took out one of Adam's ribs and created a woman from it. When Adam awoke, God presented this woman to Adam.

Adam was very pleased with his new friend. And he didn't even mind that God had made her out of his very own bone, because that meant she was like a part of him. Adam named the woman Eve, and they lived very happily in their beautiful garden home.

THE SERPENT'S LIE
Genesis 3

One day a serpent spoke to Eve. "Did God say you can't eat fruit from any of the trees in the garden?"

"No," explained Eve. "God said we could eat from all of the trees, except for the one in the middle. If we touch that tree, we will die."

"Surely you won't die," hissed the sly serpent. "It's just that God knows if you eat that sweet fruit, you will become as smart as he is."

Eve looked longingly at the ripe fruit. Then she plucked a piece from the tree and ate it.

Eve shared some of the fruit with Adam. Suddenly, they both grew embarrassed, realizing they had no clothes on. They covered themselves with leaves and hid in the bushes. God called out, "Adam, where are you?" Adam told God what they had done, and God was very sad.

God cursed the serpent for tricking Eve. He told Adam and Eve to leave the beautiful garden. From that day on, Adam would work very hard to provide food for his family and Eve would suffer great pain when giving birth to their babies. And in the end, they both would die.

CAIN AND ABEL

Genesis 4

Adam and Eve had two sons named Cain and Abel. Abel cared for the sheep, and Cain worked the fields.

One day, the two sons brought gifts to God. Abel brought a lamb, and Cain brought some grain. But when God was pleased with Abel's lamb, Cain grew very angry.

"Why are you angry, Cain?" asked God. "If you do what is right, you will be blessed." But Cain was too angry to listen. Instead, he took Abel into the field and killed him. God was disappointed with Cain. He told Cain that he could no longer make things grow. From then on, Cain would wander the earth.

Noah Builds a Boat

Genesis 6

As years passed, more people filled the earth. They no longer listened to God. Instead they spent every hour of every day thinking up ways to hurt and destroy, ways to cheat and to steal.

God grew very sad. Each time they lied or killed or hurt one another, his heart would fill with pain. Finally, God said, "I will get rid of mankind entirely. In fact, I will remove all that moves and breathes from the face of the earth."

But before God wiped the entire earth clean, he thought about his good friend, Noah.

Noah had always done what was right. Not only did Noah listen to God, but he always did whatever God told him.

So God told Noah to build an enormous ark. It would be bigger than anything that had ever been built before. Noah listened carefully as God explained how to make this ark.

Noah and his sons, Shem, Ham, and Japheth, gathered everything they needed and began to build.

THE GREAT FLOOD

Genesis 6–9

It took a long time, but finally Noah and his sons finished building the ark. Then God told Noah to load a male and female of each kind of animal onto the ark. God also told Noah to gather food for all the animals and for his family too. Enough for many days. Finally, the ark was loaded.

Then it began to rain. For forty long days it rained. It was as if all of God's sorrow was pouring down in raindrop tears. And as the waters rose, the ark began to float!

Every living thing was wiped from the earth except for Noah and his family and the animals on the ark. They floated on the waters for more than one hundred and fifty days. Finally, God began to dry the land.

But still Noah waited. Finally, God said, "Come out!"

Noah and his family and all the animals left the ark, rejoicing and thanking God. And when they looked up, they saw that God had put a promise across the sky—a rainbow! God said, "Never again will I destroy the earth."

ABRAHAM OBEYS GOD

Genesis 12

One day, a man named Abraham was told by God, "Abraham, I want you to leave your homeland and everyone you know. Go to a place I will show you. When you get there, I will bless you and make you into a great nation."

So Abraham took his wife Sarah and his nephew Lot, and set out toward the land of Canaan. They brought everything with them.

Abraham traveled wherever God told him to go. During that time God took very good care of Abraham and his family. But Abraham and Sarah were growing older, and they had no children. How could God make a man with no children into a great nation?

But one night God said, "Abraham, look up at the heavens and count the stars if you can. That is how many descendants you will have in the years to come."

In time, Abraham and Sarah did have a son, and they called him Isaac. And they thanked God for their beautiful baby boy.

Abraham and Isaac

Genesis 22

Isaac grew into a strong and healthy boy, and Abraham loved his son.

One day, God called out, "Abraham!"

"Here I am," said Abraham.

"Abraham, I want you to take your only son, Isaac, up to the mountains, and there offer him to me," said God. "I will show you where to go." Abraham felt sad. He had waited so long for a son, and he didn't want to give him away. But Abraham obeyed.

Early the next morning, he rose and took his only son up into the mountains.

After three days, Abraham reached the place God had told him about. "Father," said Isaac, "we have fire and wood, but where is the lamb for our offering?"

"God will provide," said Abraham, with tears in his eyes. And he began to carefully arrange the firewood on the altar. At last he bound Isaac and laid him on top.

"Stop!" cried a voice from the heaven. "Do not harm the boy. Now I know that you trust me completely."

Then Abraham saw a ram caught in a thicket. He and Isaac offered the ram to God. And Abraham named the mountain "God will provide."

ISAAC AND REBEKAH

Genesis 24

One day, Abraham said to his servant, "Find a good wife for Isaac."

"Shouldn't Isaac come along to pick out his bride?"

"No, Isaac must not go," said Abraham. "God has promised to increase my family. God will help you."

So the servant traveled to Abraham's homeland. When he arrived, he and his camels were very thirsty. He stopped by a spring and prayed, "God, please help me find a good wife for Isaac. When I ask a girl for a drink, let her offer to get water for all of my camels also."

Soon a beautiful girl named Rebekah came and filled her jar with water.

"Please, may I have a drink?" the servant asked.

"Certainly," she said with a smile. "And when you're done, let me also draw water for your camels." She worked hard, and then invited him to stay at her father's home. The servant told her family about Abraham and Isaac, and how he had prayed for God to show him the right woman for Isaac's wife. Rebekah's family loved her dearly, but they believed the servant. They asked Rebekah if she wanted to return with the servant to become Isaac's wife.

Rebekah said, "Yes!"

43

JACOB AND ESAU

Isaac and Rebekah were married. And Isaac loved his new wife, but for many years they had no children.

Finally, Isaac asked God to give Rebekah a baby. God answered Isaac's prayer and Rebekah became pregnant, but before her baby was born she grew concerned and asked God what was wrong. "Two nations are within you," said God. "The older will serve the younger." Then Rebekah had twins. The first was named Esau and the second, Jacob.

As the boys grew older, Esau became a skilled hunter. But Jacob preferred to stay close to home.

One evening, Jacob made stew. Esau came home and said, "Hurry up, give me some of your stew. I'm starving!"

"I'll trade you some stew for your birthright," said Jacob. "Then I'll be like the oldest."

"Fine," said Esau. "My birthright is worthless if I die from hunger!" So Esau gave Jacob his birthright.

Years later, Isaac grew blind. He knew he would soon die, so he called to Esau and said, "Go hunt some wild game, then come and prepare me a tasty meal. After that I will give you my blessing."

Rebekah heard Isaac and grew concerned. Jacob was her favorite son, and she wanted him to have Isaac's blessing.

JACOB TRICKS ESAU

Genesis 27–28

Rebekah called Jacob and told him her idea. "Hurry and bring me two goats; I'll prepare your father's favorite meal. Then you can serve it to him and get Esau's blessing."

"But he'll know I'm not Esau," said Jacob. "Esau is hairy; my skin is smooth." So Rebekah wrapped goatskins on Jacob's arms, and Jacob set the meal before Isaac. When Isaac finished eating, he gave Jacob the blessing.

When Esau discovered that Jacob had tricked him, he yelled so loudly the walls of the tent shook. He wanted to kill his brother. Rebekah begged Isaac to send Jacob to her family. Isaac agreed. But Esau was still very angry.

JACOB'S DREAM

Genesis 28

Jacob left quickly, traveling all day. When night came, he fell asleep, using a stone for a pillow. As he slept, he had a dream about a beautiful stairway that reached all the way to heaven. Angels came up and down the stairs, and God said, "I am the God of your fathers. I will give you and your children the land that you lie upon. All people will be blessed by you. I am with you and will go with you. And I will do all that I have promised."

Jacob woke up and said, "Surely God is in this place." And he made a vow to God. Then he took the stone he had slept on and set it upright to remember this special place.

JOSEPH

Genesis 37

After many long years of waiting, Jacob and his wife Rachel had a baby. It was a day of great rejoicing, and they named this son Joseph. Jacob had eleven other sons, but Joseph was his favorite son. So he made Joseph a beautiful coat with all the colors of the rainbow woven into it. One night, Joseph had an unusual dream. The next day, he told his brothers, "I dreamed we were bundling up wheat. Suddenly, my bundle of wheat rose high in the air and all of your bundles bowed down before it."

"So you must think you're better than we are," scolded his brothers. "Shall we bow down to you now?"

One day, Jacob sent Joseph to check on his brothers. They were far off, tending sheep, but they spotted him walking in the distance. "Here comes the dreamer," they said. "Let's kill him." And they began to plot against him.

"No, don't kill him," said the oldest. "Just throw him into this hole." When Joseph arrived, they jumped on him, ripped off his beautiful coat, and threw him down into a deep hole. When a band of merchants passed by, the brothers sold Joseph as a slave. They wiped animal blood on Joseph's coat and took it to their father, telling him that Joseph was dead.

JOSEPH IN EGYPT

Genesis 39–41

Joseph was taken to Egypt and sold to a man named Potiphar. Joseph worked hard, and soon Potiphar put him in charge of his entire household. But Potiphar's wife accused Joseph of betraying her husband. Although her words were false, Joseph was put in prison. But even in prison, he obeyed God. Soon he was released to help Pharaoh, the leader of all of Egypt.

"Joseph, I've heard you are able to explain dreams," said Pharaoh.

"Only with God's help," replied Joseph.

God showed Joseph what Pharaoh's dreams meant. Joseph said, "God is warning you. After seven years with plenty of food, the rains will stop. Nothing will grow for the next seven years. But if you plan, you can save your people from starvation."

"You are a wise man, Joseph," said Pharaoh. "You shall be in charge of all this." Joseph worked hard to carry out the plans that God showed him. He made sure that huge amounts of grain were stored. And when the bad years came, Egypt had plenty of food to feed its people.

A PLEA FOR HELP

Genesis 42–46

During the famine, people from all over came to Egypt for food. Even Joseph's brothers came to buy grain.

"We are the twelve sons of Jacob," they said. "But one brother is dead, and our youngest brother, Benjamin, is at home." They did not know they were speaking with Joseph.

"I think you are spies," said Joseph. "But if what you say is true, then send for this other brother."

Joseph allowed them to return to their homeland with food. But he kept one brother, and made them promise to return with Benjamin.

When he heard his sons' story, Jacob sadly agreed to let Benjamin go to Egypt. This time, Joseph invited the brothers into his home. But Joseph still didn't say who he was. Before they left, he hid a silver cup in their things. Then he sent his servant after them. "You've stolen my master's cup!" said the servant. "Benjamin must return to Egypt!"

"Please don't take him!" they cried. "Our father lost his son Joseph. It would kill him to lose Benjamin too."

At last Joseph cried out. "I am Joseph! God spared me so I could help you." He sent the brothers back home to get their father. Then he gave them a fine piece of land.

55

BABY MOSES

Exodus 1–2

Many years later, the Israelites still lived in Egypt. A new Egyptian pharaoh had made them into slaves, but the number of Israelites continued to grow. So the evil pharaoh ordered that all Israelite baby boys be thrown into the Nile River.

One Hebrew mother could not bear to drown her beautiful baby boy. So she wove a sturdy basket in the shape of a tiny boat and made it watertight. Then she kissed her baby and set his basket afloat in the reeds along the Nile River.

Later that day, the princess was by the river and heard the baby's cries in the reeds. "Bring me that basket," she said to her handmaidens. The baby's sister, Miriam, waited nearby. "Poor little thing," said the princess. "He must be a Hebrew baby."

"Shall I fetch a Hebrew woman to care for him?" asked Miriam. The princess agreed, and Miriam ran home and got her mother. The baby boy was spared! And his very own mother took care of him.

"I shall name him Moses," said the princess, "for I took him up out of the water." And she raised him as her very own son.

MOSES RUNS AWAY

Exodus 2–3

When Moses was a man, he saw an Egyptian beating a Hebrew slave. So he struck and killed the Egyptian. The next day, Moses saw two Hebrews fighting. "Why do you hurt your brother?" he asked.

"Why do you judge us?" demanded one of the men. "Didn't you just kill a fellow Egyptian?" Moses realized that his secret was out, so he ran away to Midian. There he became a shepherd. One day, as he tended sheep, he saw a bush that was on fire. But even though the flames leaped high, the bush didn't burn up. Moses drew closer.

"Moses! Moses!" called God. "Stay right there, and take off your sandals, for the ground where you stand is holy. I am the God of your people." Moses fell to his knees and hid his face in fear.

"I have seen my people suffering," said God. "I have come to deliver them out of Egypt and into a land that flows with milk and honey. And you, Moses will go to Pharaoh. You will lead my people out of Egypt!"

"Why me?" asked Moses.

"Because I am with you," said God. "Go and tell Pharaoh to let my people go."

Moses obeyed God. He gathered his family and returned to Egypt. He stood before Pharaoh, with his brother Aaron at his side. God used Moses and Aaron to perform fantastic miracles. But Pharaoh refused to listen to God.

PLAGUES, PLAGUES, AND MORE PLAGUES

Exodus 4–12

Moses met with Pharaoh. "Because you will not listen to God and let his people go, God will turn your river into blood." When Moses' staff touched the Nile every drop of water turned to blood. But even after seven days Pharaoh still refused to listen.

So God sent another plague. The river grew thick with frogs. The frogs overflowed the banks and covered the ground. Pharaoh begged Moses to send the frogs away. He even promised to let God's people go. But when God got rid of the frogs, Pharaoh broke his promise.

And so God sent more plagues. There were huge swarms of gnats. Then millions of flies. And once again Pharaoh promised to let God's people go. But when the pests were gone, Pharaoh said, "NO!" Then the Egyptian animals died and Egyptians became covered in horrible, itching sores. Then God sent locusts, and hail, and three days of darkness. But Pharaoh's heart remained hard.

Finally, God told Moses, "I will send one last plague. To protect my people, you must mark your homes with lamb's blood. When I pass over Egypt, I will spare the homes with this mark. But all firstborn sons in the unmarked homes will die." God did as he said. Many Egyptians died, including Pharaoh's own son. But the Israelites were spared. At last, Pharaoh shouted, "GO!"

MOSES LEADS HIS PEOPLE

Exodus 12–15

It was the middle of the night when Moses led the Israelites out of Egypt.

The Egyptians called out to the Israelites, "Hurry! Hurry! You must leave quickly before we all die!"

As the Israelites left, Egyptians gave them gold and silver. The Egyptians were weary from the plagues and hoped that God would now have mercy on Egypt.

God led his people as they traveled. In the daytime, he gave a pillar of cloud to follow. At night, he gave a pillar of fire. Finally, Moses stopped at the banks of the Red Sea and waited for God.

Meanwhile, back in Egypt, Pharaoh changed his mind again! He gathered his army. He wanted to capture the Israelites.

When the Israelites saw the army in the distance, they grew terrified. "Moses!" they cried. "Did you bring us out to the desert so we could be killed by Pharaoh?"

"Don't be afraid," said Moses. "Watch and see what God is able to do!"

Then Moses reached out his hand over the Red Sea. God pushed aside the waters, and blew a mighty wind that divided the sea in half! The Israelites all walked straight into the sea but each step they took landed upon dry ground.

Pharaoh's army entered the parted sea the same as the Israelites had done. But God made the walls of water fall, thundering back into the sea!

As the Israelites watched Pharaoh's army being buried by the Red Sea, they knew their God was very powerful. They trusted him. And they trusted Moses.

63

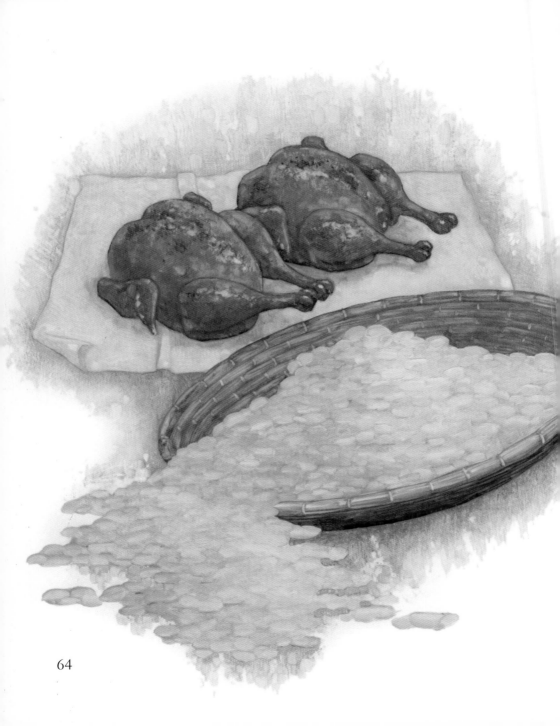

FOOD FROM HEAVEN

Exodus 16

After crossing the Red Sea, the Israelites entered the desert. But God took care of them. Still, it wasn't long before they forgot about God and began to grumble. "We were better off in Egypt," they complained. "We had good food there."

Then God told Moses he would drop food from the sky just like rain. "Tell everyone to gather bread each morning and meat each evening," said God.

The next morning, the ground was coated with white flakes of bread that tasted as sweet as honey. They called it manna. In the evening, quail covered the ground for their meat. God sent them this food the whole time they were in the wilderness.

WATER IN THE DESERT

Exodus 17

Moses continued to lead the Israelites through the desert. Once again they began to grumble. "Moses, why did you bring us out here?" they demanded. "It's too hot! Do you want us to die of thirst?"

Moses cried out to God, "What will I do about these people?" Then God told Moses what to do.

Moses did as God said. He chose some older leaders to go with him, and they walked until they reached a certain rock. When Moses struck the rock with his staff, fresh, cool water gushed out just like a fountain. And once again the people were happy.

Ten Commandments

Exodus 19–20

One day, God called Moses to the top of Mount Sinai. There he gave Moses a set of ten rules for God's people to live by.

I alone am God; worship no one but me.

Do not worship things.

Say my name only when you want me to listen.

Set aside one day each week to rest.

Respect your parents.

Do not take a human life.

Do not break a marriage vow.

Do not steal.

Do not lie.

Do not envy what is not yours.

Twelve Explorers

Numbers 13–14

God said to Moses, "Choose a man from each tribe of Israel, then send them to explore the land of Canaan. I will give you this land." So Moses picked twelve men, and they set off.

They soon discovered Canaan was a land flowing with milk and honey. The men found many delicious fruits to bring back. It took two men just to carry one gigantic cluster of grapes!

After forty days, the explorers returned. "It's a great place!" some said. "There's lots of food. But the people who live there are powerful."

"Wait!" cried an explorer named Caleb. "God has already promised to give us Canaan. We just need to go in and get what is ours."

An explorer named Joshua cried out, "Listen to Caleb! That land flows with milk and honey. God wants us to have it. Just have faith!"

But it was too late. The Israelites were angry and refused to listen. Instead they complained again.

God was sad when he saw how they turned against him after all the miracles he had done.

"I will forgive them," God told Moses. "But no one who doubted will set one foot into Canaan."

When Moses told the people what God had said, they were sorry. They started to walk toward Canaan, thinking that they could still have that land. "It's too late now," warned Moses. "God gave you your chance, and you doubted him."

71

JERICHO

Joshua 1–6

After Moses died God said to Joshua, "Lead my people across the Jordan River. Each place you set your foot will be yours. I am with you wherever you go."

So Joshua sent two men ahead to spy on a town called Jericho. When they got there, they stayed with a woman named Rahab, who hid them when they were in danger. When it grew dark, she helped them escape.

Rahab asked, "Please promise me that you will not hurt my family when your people take Jericho."

God told Joshua exactly what to do in order to take the city of Jericho. First, Joshua gathered men into an army to march around the city. Then came seven priests with ram's horn trumpets. Behind the priests came the ark of the covenant, and following the ark came more armed guards.

They paraded around Jericho one time each day for six days. During this time, the priests blew on the trumpets.

On the seventh day, the Israelites paraded around Jericho six times. The priests blew their trumpets.

On the seventh time around the city, Joshua called out a signal. Everyone yelled with all their might!

At that noise, the walls of Jericho fell. All who were inside the city ran in fear except for the woman Rahab. She knew she would be safe. And she was.

GIDEON

Judges 6–7

Long after the battle of Jericho, the Israelites forgot to obey God again. They hid out in the hills, fearing the Midianites. One day, a man named Gideon heard an angel say, "God is with you, mighty warrior!"

"God is with me?" asked Gideon. "Then why are we having such troubles?"

"You shall save Israel," said the angel. "For God has chosen you to lead your people."

"Me?" cried Gideon. "But who will listen to me? I am no one!"

"God will go with you," said the angel.

Thousands of men came to help Gideon. But God said, "That's too many. Send back any who are afraid." So Gideon let 22,000 men leave. Now 10,000 remained.

"You still have too many," said God. He showed Gideon whom to send home. Now, only 300 men remained. God told Gideon's army to surround the Midianite camp. When Gideon gave the signal, they smashed jars, waved torches, yelled loudly, and blew their trumpets. The startled Midianites grabbed their swords and fought against themselves. Then they ran. God used Gideon's tiny army to win the battle.

Samson

Judges 13–16

After Gideon died, Israel forgot to obey God. Soon they were captured by the Philistines, a people who hated God. One day, an angel appeared to an Israelite woman telling her she would have a son who would save Israel from the Philistines.

When the woman's son was born, she named him Samson. He grew up to be the strongest man ever!

For years, Samson battled the Philistines. One time, he fought an army and when the fight ended, Samson killed 1,000 Philistines with the jawbone of a donkey!

Samson loved a woman named Delilah, who really worked for the Philistines. "Why are you so strong, Samson?" she asked. And although she begged, Samson wouldn't tell. Finally, she cried, "You don't love me, Samson, or you would share your secret."

"It's my vow to God," he whispered. "If my hair is cut, my strength will go." When he fell asleep, the Philistines cut his hair. Samson's strength was gone. The Philistines bound and blinded him. Later they threw a big party. But Samson prayed. And God gave him strength to push and collapse their temple. That day, thousands of Philistines died along with Samson.

Ruth and Naomi

Ruth

Naomi lived far from her homeland. Her husband and sons had died. All she had left were her two daughters-in-law. One day, Naomi told them, "I am returning to my homeland."

"Please, Naomi," begged Ruth, one of the daughters-in-law. "Let me go where you go. Your people will be my people. And your God will be my God." So the two women traveled to Bethlehem.

"It's time for the barley harvest, Naomi," said Ruth. "If I gather leftover grain, we can make bread to eat." So Ruth picked up grain missed by the harvesters.

A man named Boaz owned the field and wondered who she was. "She came back with old Naomi," said his foreman. "All day long she has worked hard."

Boaz called Ruth and said, "Gather as much grain as you need, and my workers will watch for you."

"You are very kind to a foreigner," she said.

"You helped my relative Naomi," said Boaz. "May God bless you."

One night, Naomi told Ruth to go to the threshing floor where Boaz was sleeping. She told Ruth to wait for him there. "What are you doing here?" he asked.

"Naomi has sent me," said Ruth. "Since you are her nearest relative, I have come to ask you to care for us."

"I will take care of you," said Boaz.

Naomi rejoiced. And Ruth became the great-grandmother of the great King David!

HANNAH'S PRAYER

1 Samuel 1

Hannah loved God. But she was sad, for she had no children. Each year, her husband took her to a place called Shiloh, and Hannah prayed a special prayer that God would give her a child. One year, she prayed, "Dear God, if you will only give me a son, I will give him back to you, to serve you all his days." She prayed so hard her mouth moved, but no words came out. A priest asked if she was drunk. "No," she said. "I'm pouring my heart out to God."

"May you find favor in God's eyes," said the priest.

The following year, Hannah's prayers were answered. She had a baby boy named Samuel!

She happily cared for Samuel until he was old enough to leave her. Then she kept her promise to God and took Samuel to live with the priests in Shiloh.

God gave Hannah many more children. And Hannah was pleased to know that Samuel was growing up in Shiloh, where he would love and serve God always.

SAMUEL

1 Samuel 3, 8

One night, Samuel heard a voice calling. He thought it was the old priest Eli, but Eli said, "I didn't call you; go back and lie down." Samuel heard the call again, but Eli still said it wasn't him. When Samuel heard it the third time, Eli said, "It must be God. Go back and listen." So Samuel went back, and God spoke.

But Samuel didn't want to tell Eli what God had said, because God was very unhappy with Eli's sons.

"Do not hide God's words from me," said Eli. And so Samuel told Eli. From then on Samuel always said what God told him to say.

Samuel continued to serve God. Israel knew Samuel was a man they could trust to speak God's words. People all over Israel respected Samuel. And for a while, Israel lived in peace. Samuel helped them to remember to listen to God.

When Samuel grew old, the people of Israel said they wanted a king. Samuel felt bad and told God, and God said, "They aren't rejecting you, Samuel. They are rejecting me." For until then, God had been their king.

KING SAUL

1 Samuel 9

Samuel warned Israel that getting a king would bring problems, but the people would not listen. They wanted to be like all the other countries who had kings.

One day, a young man named Saul and his servant were out looking for a herd of lost donkeys. They went for miles and miles, and finally Saul wanted to go back home. But the servant said, "There is a prophet in this town. Maybe he can tell us where the donkeys are." So Saul and the servant went to see Samuel.

God had told Samuel the day before that a stranger would come to town—the man chosen by God to rule Israel. Samuel met Saul and said, "I am the one you're looking for. Your donkeys have been found. Now, God wants to bless you and your family." Then Samuel invited Saul to an important dinner.

The next morning, Samuel poured oil on Saul's head and said, "God has chosen you to lead his people. God's spirit will come upon you and help you." After Saul left, all that Samuel said took place. And Saul became the first king of Israel.

85

DAVID

1 Samuel 16

King Saul disobeyed God. God then told Samuel to find a new king. This time, God showed Samuel a boy named David who tended sheep for his father. God said, "I don't look at the outside of a person, I look at the heart." So Samuel poured oil on David's head to show that he would be the next king of Israel.

Later on, when King Saul couldn't sleep at night, he asked for a musician to play for him. His servant said, "There is a young man who plays beautiful harp music. He is a brave young man who loves God." So David came and played his harp for the king, and Saul was pleased with David and his music.

David and Goliath

1 Samuel 17

One day, David delivered food to his brothers who were battling the Philistines. He heard a Philistine shouting and making fun of them.

"Who is that man?" asked David. They told him about Goliath the mighty warrior. But David wasn't afraid of the giant. When King Saul heard of David's bravery, he called David before him.

"Don't worry, I'll go fight that giant," said David.

"But he's a warrior," said Saul. "You're only a boy."

"God will help me kill this giant," said David.

Saul gave David his armor and weapons. But they were too big for David.

So without any armor, David faced the giant. He stopped by a stream to pick up some stones. Then he stood before Goliath.

"Am I a dog that you come at me with sticks?" bellowed Goliath.

David looked up and said, "You come against me with weapons, but I come against you in the name of the Lord Almighty." Then David put a stone in his sling and swung it around until the sling whistled. The stone whizzed through the air and smacked Goliath right in the forehead. And the giant fell to the ground.

DAVID THE KING

2 Samuel 1–7

When Saul died, David became the new king of Israel. David led the Israelites through many victorious battles against their enemies. Before long, David conquered Jerusalem and it was called the City of David. He then built a palace there.

The Israelites rejoiced when David and his men brought the Ark of God into the City of David. And King David danced in the streets, praising God!

With all their enemies defeated, Israel enjoyed a time of peace. David loved God, and his greatest wish was to build a temple for God. But David didn't always obey God. So finally God told David that David's son would be the one to build God's temple.

While David was king, he wrote many beautiful songs. Most were to praise God, but some were to say he was sorry. David loved to worship God with his songs.

SOLOMON

1 Kings 3–9

After King David died his son, Solomon, became Israel's king.

One night, God appeared to King Solomon in a dream. "Ask for whatever you want," said God.

"You did so much for my father," said Solomon. "His kingdom was great. But now I am king and I feel like a little child. I don't know how to rule. So please make my heart wise so that I can do what is right for your people." God was glad that Solomon didn't ask for riches or long life. God granted King Solomon's wish, and Solomon became the wisest man ever. God also gave Solomon a long life and great riches.

Just as God had promised David, Solomon built God's temple. It took seven years to complete the beautiful building. Skilled craftsman decorated it with carved wood and fine gold.

When it was finished, Solomon held a huge celebration. For fourteen days the people worshiped God at the temple. Although the temple was wonderful, Solomon knew that it was not great enough to contain the Almighty God. But God promised Solomon that his eyes and his heart would always be on the temple and with his people.

ELIJAH

1 Kings 17

After King Solomon died, many kings ruled Israel. Some were good, some were bad. King Ahab was very bad. He turned his back on God.

During King Ahab's time, there was a man called Elijah who listened to God and spoke for God. He was a prophet.

One day, Elijah told King Ahab, "God has shown me there will be no rain for the next few years unless I say so." Then Elijah went off to hide in a place that God showed him. Each day, God sent ravens to carry meat and bread for Elijah to eat. The birds came in the morning and the evening. And Elijah drank water from the stream.

A Fiery Test

1 Kings 18

After three years, God told Elijah to speak to the wicked king. "Ahab," said Elijah, "you've turned from God, and you serve the false god Baal. Now let's see whose God is real!"

So Ahab's false prophets made an altar with wood piled high. "Can your gods make your wood burn?" asked Elijah. Ahab's false prophets danced and shouted, but their altar did not burn. "Perhaps your gods are asleep," said Elijah. "Or maybe they've taken a trip."

Then Elijah made an altar for God. He piled it high with wood and poured gallons of water on it. Elijah prayed, and the altar burst into fiery flames!

The people cried out, "The Lord God—he is God!"

ELIJAH AND ELISHA

1 Kings 19, 2 Kings 2

God chose a man named Elisha to follow Elijah faithfully. But one day, Elijah said, "Elisha, you stay here. God is sending me away."

"As God lives, I will never leave you," said Elisha, and he continued to stay with Elijah. Each time Elijah told Elisha to stay behind, Elisha refused to leave his friend.

"What can I do for you before I go?" asked Elijah.

"I want a double share of your spirit," said Elisha.

Then a chariot of fire swept down from heaven and took Elijah away. But God answered Elisha's request, and like his friend, Elisha became a powerful prophet.

Elisha helps Naaman

2 Kings 5

Naaman was a good man who commanded an army in Aram. But Naaman had a problem. He had a disease called leprosy.

"Naaman should go see the great prophet Elisha," said a Hebrew girl who worked for Naaman's wife. "Elisha could heal Naaman."

So Naaman gathered rich gifts and set off for Israel. When he finally reached Elisha's house, Elisha didn't even come out. Instead he sent a messenger to Naaman. "Go and bathe in the Jordan River seven times," said the servant. "And then you will be healed." But Naaman didn't like this message.

"I could have stayed home and bathed in my own river!" said Naaman. "I expected more from this prophet."

But Naaman's servants convinced him to try. When Naaman came out of the water the seventh time, he was completely healed.

Naaman said to Elisha, "Your God is the only true God. Please accept these gifts as my thanks."

"As the Lord lives, I will not," said Elisha. So Naaman went on his way, but Elisha's servant followed him. The servant lied to Naaman and took the gifts. When the servant returned, Elisha knew everything.

"Because of your dishonesty," said Elisha to the servant, "you will now have Naaman's leprosy."

QUEEN ESTHER

Esther

King Xerxes ruled Persia. When he needed a wife, his servants searched the land for the most beautiful women. A beautiful woman named Esther was chosen. She was good and wise. But she was an Israelite. A kind relative named Mordecai warned her not to tell anyone she was an Israelite.

When King Xerxes saw Esther, he was very pleased. He set the royal crown on her head, and she became his wife and queen.

Mordecai often sat by the palace gates to hear how Esther was doing. One time, he overheard men plotting to kill the king. Mordecai warned Esther, and she told the king. The bad men were arrested, and Mordecai's good deed was written in the king's record book.

Later, a powerful man named Haman became angry at Mordecai. Haman knew that Mordecai was an Israelite, and he encouraged King Xerxes to make it legal to kill Israelites.

Esther knew this law meant that she too could die. "I will do all I can to change this," she said to Mordecai. "Please ask my people to pray for me."

And Mordecai did.

Esther went to speak to the king. King Xerxes asked, "What can I do for you, dear Queen? I will give you whatever you ask, up to half my kingdom."

"I have prepared a banquet for you and Haman. I would like you to be my guests," said Esther.

So the king and Haman came and enjoyed a delicious meal served by Esther. "Now, dear Queen, tell me what it is I can do for you," said King Xerxes.

"If you both could come for another feast tomorrow," said Esther, "then I will tell you my request."

The next day, King Xerxes and Haman came to another fine banquet. "Now, tell me, my Queen, what is your request?" said King Xerxes.

"Dear King," said Esther. "If you are pleased with me, I beg you to spare my life. And also spare the lives of my people. It seems unfair that we are to be put to death."

"Who dares to do this?" demanded the king.

"It is this cruel Haman," said Esther, pointing to her enemy. The king ordered Haman to be hung that very same day.

Esther and her people were safe.

THE FIERY FURNACE

Daniel 3

Many years later, Israel was defeated by the Babylonians and taken captive.

The king of Babylon's workers had built a giant golden statue. The king made a law commanding everyone to bow down and worship the statue whenever they heard the king's special music.

But Shadrach, Meshach, and Abednego were Israelites. They refused to worship the statue. They would only worship the one true God.

So the king ordered that these young men be thrown into a huge fiery furnace. But first he said, "Make the fire seven times hotter than usual!"

The king watched as they were thrown into the furnace. "Weren't only three men thrown into the fire?" asked the king. "I see four men," he said, "and one of them looks like a god!" The king approached the furnace. "Shadrach, Meshach, Abednego!" he yelled. "Servants of the Most High God, come out!"

So the three came out. Nothing on them was burnt, and they didn't even smell of smoke.

"Your God is great!" cried the king. "He sent his angel to rescue you. From now on, no one will be allowed to say anything bad about your God."

DANIEL AND THE LIONS

Daniel 6

King Darius ruled Babylon for a time. King Darius respected Daniel. He knew Daniel was a godly man who had served the kings before him. But some of King Darius' men did not like Daniel. They wanted to get rid of him. So they convinced the king to make a law forbidding people to pray to anyone but the king. Anyone who broke this law would be thrown into the lions' den.

Daniel knew about the law, but he continued to pray to God. The men spied on Daniel and told the king that Daniel had broken the law.

The king sadly agreed, and Daniel was put into the lions' den.

"May your God rescue you," said the king. That night, the king could not eat or sleep. He was too worried about Daniel.

Early the next morning, he ran out to the lions' den.

"Daniel!" he cried. "Has your God been able to rescue you from the hungry lions?"

"King Darius," called Daniel, "may you live forever. Yes, my God sent his angel to shut the lions' mouths! They have not hurt me." Then King Darius had the evil men thrown into the lions' den. And this time, God did not close the lions' mouths.

107

JONAH AND THE BIG FISH

Jonah 1–3

"Jonah," said God, "go to Nineveh and tell them I've seen their wickedness."

But Jonah didn't like the people of Nineveh. He thought he could run away from God. So he got on a ship sailing away from Nineveh.

Soon a storm came. The wind roared and the waves crashed around the ship.

Finally, Jonah realized he was the reason for the terrible storm. "Throw me overboard," said Jonah, "and the storm will end."

The sailors didn't want to throw Jonah out, but they agreed. They threw Jonah into the sea. Instantly, the sea became calm.

Then God sent a gigantic fish to swallow Jonah. For three days and three nights, Jonah stayed inside the fish. While he was inside the fish, he asked God to help him.

Finally, God made the fish spit Jonah out onto dry land. This time, Jonah obeyed God. He went straight to Nineveh and began to preach.

"God has seen your wickedness," said Jonah. "He will destroy Nineveh in forty days."

The people listened to Jonah. They were sorry for the bad things they had done. They began to pray. They returned to God, and God did not destroy them.

New Testament

AN ANGEL'S VISIT

Luke 1

One day an angel appeared to a young woman named Mary. "God is happy with you," said the angel. "You have been chosen to have a baby boy. You will call him Jesus, and he will be great. He will be the Son of the Most High!"

Mary stared at the angel. "How can this be?" she asked.

"God will send his Holy Spirit to give you this baby," said the angel. "And God has done another miracle. After many years of waiting, God will give your relatives Elizabeth and Zechariah a son. See, nothing is impossible with God."

Mary bowed. "I am God's humble servant. I will do all that you have said." Then the angel left.

Mary visits Elizabeth

Luke 1

Mary quickly left to go visit Elizabeth. Elizabeth met her at the door with a big smile. "Mary!" Elizabeth cried with joy. "When I heard your voice, the baby inside me leaped! Now I must ask you—why has the mother of my Lord come to see me?"

Mary was amazed that Elizabeth already knew what God was doing. Mary stayed with Elizabeth for several months before she returned to her home.

116

Joseph's Dream

Matthew 1

Mary was engaged to marry a man named Joseph. But he was upset. Joseph did not understand why Mary was to have a baby before they were married.

Then one night, an angel appeared to Joseph in a dream. The angel said, "Joseph, do not be afraid to take Mary as your wife. For God has chosen her and blessed her to give birth to his very own Son. This child shall be called Jesus, and he will save his people from sin."

TO BETHLEHEM AND A STABLE

Luke 2

In those days, a law was passed that everyone must travel to their hometown to have their names written down. Although Mary was almost ready to have her baby, she and Joseph had to go to Bethlehem.

After a long, tiring journey, they reached the small town. Mary knew it was time for God's Son to be born. She was very weary from traveling and wanted a place to rest. But many people bustled through the crowded streets—they too had come to record their names. And although Joseph searched the whole town, he could not find a room for them to stay in.

At last, Joseph found a shelter for Mary to rest. It was only a stable for oxen, cattle, and donkeys. Yet, it was exactly the right spot, the very place God had chosen. Before long, Mary gave birth to God's only Son.

Mary wrapped sweet baby Jesus in clean strips of soft cloth. Then she gently laid him upon the straw in a wooden manger, the very same manger that the oxen and cows had eaten from.

THE SHEPHERDS' SURPRISE!

Luke 2

Shepherds were caring for sheep on a hillside. Suddenly, an angel appeared before them. "Don't be afraid," said the angel. "God has sent me to tell you the greatest news! This very day, a Savior is born in the city of David! You will find him lying in a manger."

Then the night burst into brilliant light and angels filled the sky. "Glory to God!" they shouted. "Peace on earth! Good will to all mankind!"

The shepherds left the hillside and went down to Bethlehem. And just as the angels had said, they found baby Jesus lying in a manger.

WISE MEN FROM THE EAST

Matthew 2

Some time after Jesus was born, wise men journeyed to Jerusalem. They had learned that a King had been born in that region. They stopped at King Herod's palace. "Where is this newborn King?" asked the wise men. "We have seen his star and know that he is to be King of the Jews. We want to worship him." But King Herod did not want to share his throne with anyone.

King Herod called in priests and scribes. "What do the prophets say about a King like this?" he demanded.

"The Scriptures say a very special King will be born in the town of Bethlehem," explained the men. "And he will be a shepherd to God's people."

Then King Herod called back the wise men and told them to seek this King in Bethlehem. "And when you find him," said King Herod, "you must return and tell me where he is, so I too can worship him." But the truth was, King Herod did not wish to worship Jesus—he wanted to kill him.

The wise men traveled to Bethlehem and found Mary, Joseph, and baby Jesus. They worshiped Jesus and presented valuable gifts of gold, frankincense, and myrrh. An angel warned the wise men not to return to Herod's palace to tell the evil king about baby Jesus. He also warned Joseph to flee from Bethlehem.

And so Joseph quickly took Mary and Jesus to Egypt, where they stayed until it was safe to return.

JESUS VISITS HIS FATHER'S HOUSE

Luke 2

When Jesus was twelve, he traveled with his parents and other friends and relatives to Jerusalem to celebrate the Passover. When the celebration was finished, the group began their journey back home. But after many miles, Mary and Joseph realized that Jesus was not with them.

"Jesus, where are you?" cried Mary and Joseph as they searched. They hurried back to Jerusalem. For three days, they searched.

Finally, Mary and Joseph stopped at the temple. There was Jesus! He was sitting with the teachers, listening and asking them questions. All who heard Jesus speak were astonished at his wisdom. Mary ran up to him. "Jesus!" she cried. "Your father and I have been looking all over for you!"

"Didn't you know I would be in my Father's house?" he asked.

Mary and Joseph did not understand exactly what Jesus meant by this, but they all traveled happily back home. And Jesus continued to grow into a man who was loved and respected by both God and men.

125

JESUS IS BAPTIZED

Matthew 3

Many years later, John the Baptist began to preach around Judea. He wore a garment made of camel's hair and ate grasshoppers and wild honey for food. "Repent," he cried. "And stop doing wrong! God's Kingdom is coming soon!" People from miles around came to hear John preach. And hundreds prayed, telling God they were sorry for their sin. Then John baptized them in the Jordan River.

"I baptize with water," John explained to the crowds. "But a greater One is coming! He will baptize you with the Holy Spirit—and with fire!"

Jesus traveled to the place where John was preaching. He asked John to baptize him. "I, baptize you?" cried John. "I am not fit to carry your sandals. You should baptize me!"

"Please," said Jesus. "It is right for you to do so." And so John obeyed Jesus.

As Jesus rose from the water, the heavens split open and God's Spirit landed upon Jesus in the form of a beautiful dove. A voice spoke from heaven. "This is my beloved Son, and I am very pleased with him!"

TEMPTED IN THE WILDERNESS

Matthew 4

After his baptism, Jesus spent time alone with God in the wilderness. For forty days, he ate no food. He grew very hungry. "Jesus," called a voice, "if you are really God's Son, why don't you turn these stones into bread so that you can eat?"

Jesus recognized Satan's voice, and he said, "It is written, 'Man does not live by eating only bread, but by every word that comes from God's mouth.'"

Then Satan showed Jesus the peak of the temple and said, "If you are really God's Son, you could jump from here and scripture says angels would catch you."

"It also says, 'Do not tempt God,'" answered Jesus.

Then Satan took Jesus to the top of a tall mountain and said, "Look down there. See all that lies below you. Bow down and worship me, and I will give it all to you."

"Get away from me, Satan!" commanded Jesus. "It is written, 'Worship God alone, and serve only him.'"

At that, Satan fled, and angels came down and cared for Jesus.

"Come follow me"

Mark 1–3

One day, Jesus walked along the sandy shore next to the Sea of Galilee. Many fishermen were working at the water's edge. Jesus called out, "Simon and Andrew! Come follow me, and I will teach you to fish for men." The two brothers instantly left their nets and joined Jesus.

The three walked along until Jesus saw two more fishermen, who were also brothers. "James and John," he called, "come follow me." And these men left their boats and went with Jesus.

Jesus saw a man named Levi, who was later called Matthew, working at his tax office. Jesus called out, "Levi, come follow me!" And Levi stood up, left the office, and followed Jesus. Later, Jesus went to Levi's house for a meal. But no one liked tax collectors, and the religious leaders questioned why Jesus would eat with someone like Levi and his sinful friends.

But Jesus said, "Healthy people don't need to see a doctor. I came to call sinners, not those who already think they are good."

Then Jesus chose seven more men to follow him. That gave him twelve disciples altogether.

JESUS' FIRST MIRACLE

John 2

Jesus and his disciples went to a wedding in Cana. Jesus' mother, Mary, was also there. "Jesus," whispered Mary, "there's a problem. They have run out of wine to serve the wedding guests."

"Why are you telling me this?" asked Jesus.

Mary called the servants over. "Do whatever Jesus says," she instructed them.

Jesus then pointed to six large water jugs. "Fill those with water," he said.

The servants filled the jugs with water then stood before Jesus expectantly. "Now," said Jesus, pointing to a jug, "dip some out and present it to the master of this banquet." The servants did just as Jesus said.

The master tasted it. He took the bridegroom aside and said, "Usually they serve the finest wine at the beginning of the wedding celebration. But you, you have saved the very best for last!"

Jesus' disciples were amazed by this miracle! Who was this man? And they all decided to put their faith in him.

MOUNTAINTOP TEACHING
Matthew 5–6

One day, Jesus took his disciples to a quiet mountainside.

"You are the light of the world!" he said to them. "A city on a hill is hard to hide. And when you light a lamp, do you put a bucket on top of it? No, of course not! You set it on a table so the whole house is lit by it.

"Let your life shine like a bright light so others will praise God the Father for the good he is doing in you!"

Jesus warned them, "Be careful when you help people or give to those in need. Make sure you do it quietly and from your heart. Don't make a big show so people will praise you. And when you pray, don't use fancy words and talk loudly. But pray in a quiet place."

Jesus taught them this prayer:

Dear Father in heaven,

Your name is the most holy.

Let your kingdom rule,

let your will be done,

on earth just like in heaven.

Give us what we need for today.

Forgive us when we do wrong,

and help us to forgive others who do wrong.

Lead us far away from what tempts us,

and save us from evil.

Your kingdom and power and glory will last forever!

Amen.

THE STORY OF THE SEEDS

Mark 4

Jesus said, "There once was a farmer who went out to plant seeds. Some seeds fell on the hard-packed footpath, and hungry birds came and gobbled them up. Other seeds fell into a rocky place where there was no good soil for roots. The plants sprang up anyway but the sun came out and they withered and died.

"Then some seeds fell among the weeds and they grew. Before long the weeds choked out the good plants so they never produced any grain. And finally some of the seeds were planted into the good, healthy soil. These plants grew up strong and tall, and produced a good crop."

But the people didn't understand the story. Later, Jesus explained it to his disciples.

"You see, the seeds are like God's Word. Some people hear God's Word, but Satan steals it away—just like the hungry birds. Other people are like the seeds that sprang up quickly in the rocky soil—they are excited and joyful at first, but their faith isn't deep. When troubles come they have no strength, they're like the plants that withered in the sun.

"Then there are those who hear God's Word, but worry about getting rich. Their worries crowd out the truth – the same way the weeds crowded out the good plants.

"But finally," continued Jesus, "there are those people whose hearts are eager and ready to hear God's Word. They are like good healthy soil, and God's Word can make deep roots in them."

137

THE CENTURION'S FAITH

Matthew 8

Jesus went to a town called Capernaum. There he met a worried centurion.

"Lord," said the centurion, "my servant is very sick."

"I will go and heal him," said Jesus.

"Oh no, Lord," said the centurion. "I don't deserve to have you come to my house. But I know if you just say the word, my servant will be healed."

Jesus was astonished at the centurion's words. He turned and spoke to the people around him.

"The truth is I have never found anyone in all of Israel with such great faith!"

Jesus turned to the centurion. "Go, right now! Your servant will be healed just as you have believed he would."

And when the centurion arrived home, his servant was completely well!

A Frightening Storm

Luke 8

One day Jesus said to his disciples, "Let's go over to the other side of the lake."

So they climbed into a boat and began to sail across the water. Jesus soon fell asleep. While he was sleeping, a huge and horrible storm began to rage.

High waves smashed with fury into the boat, and the wind howled and screamed. The boat was tossed back and forth with each new wave. Soon they were almost sinking. The disciples knew they were in danger and feared for their lives. But all the while, Jesus slept peacefully.

"Master!" the disciples cried out in despair. "Help us! We are surely going to drown!"

Jesus got up from his nap and told the wind and waves to be still. Immediately all grew calm.

"What has happened to your faith?" Jesus asked his disciples. But they were so surprised when the storm stopped that they couldn't even answer him.

Later they whispered to each other in amazement, "Who can this man possibly be? Even the wind and waves obey him!"

Feeding the Crowds

John 6

Jesus and his disciples took a boat across the Sea of Galilee, for Jesus wished to get away from the busy towns. But as they sailed, they spotted a huge crowd walking along the shore. When the boat reached the other side, Jesus saw this crowd coming toward them. He turned to Philip and said, "Where shall we buy food for these people?"

Philip looked up in surprise. "It would take a fortune to feed all these people!"

"Here's a boy who's willing to share," announced Andrew. "He has five loaves of bread and two little fish. That won't feed many people."

"Tell everyone to sit down," said Jesus. Soon the huge crowd was seated on the green, grassy slope. Jesus thanked God for the boy's lunch. Then he broke the bread and fish and gave it to the crowd. Everyone ate.

"Now," said Jesus, "gather all the leftovers, and be sure not to waste any." The disciples filled twelve baskets of leftovers. And the crowd was amazed!

143

144

HE WALKS ON WATER

Matthew 14

Jesus needed time with his Father. So he went to the hills to pray.

As the sun set, the disciples began to sail across the lake. But when it became dark, the wind began to stir the waves, tossing the small boat back and forth. Then in the middle of the night, the disciples noticed something strange. A man walked toward them right on top of the water.

"It's a ghost!" they cried in terror.

"Don't be afraid!" called Jesus. "It is I."

Peter yelled, "If it's you, Lord, call me out to you!" Jesus called, and Peter climbed out of the boat. He too began to walk on the water. But when his eyes looked away from Jesus and down at the frothing sea, Peter began to sink. "Help me, Lord!" he cried. Jesus grabbed Peter's hand.

"Peter, where's your faith?" asked Jesus as they climbed into the boat.

But Peter and the other disciples could only bow down before Jesus. "You really are the Son of God!" they said.

A GOOD NEIGHBOR

Luke 10

Jesus told this story to teach what it really means to love your neighbor as yourself:

"One day, a Jewish man was traveling from Jerusalem to Jericho," began Jesus. "But he was attacked by robbers. They stole his clothes and money. And they left him beside the road to die.

"After a while, a Jewish priest came along. He saw the poor, beaten man. But the priest did not want to be bothered. So he turned his head and went to the other side of the road. He continued on his way. Later on, a Levite came along. He too saw the bleeding man next to the road, but he did exactly the same as the priest. Then a Samaritan came along," continued Jesus.

The people listened closely, knowing that Jews and Samaritans never got along.

"When this Samaritan saw the injured man, he felt sorry for him. He stopped, and cleaned and bandaged the man's wounds. Then he lifted the man onto his donkey and took him to a nearby inn. There, he cared for the man. The next day, the Samaritan had to be on his way, but he left money with the innkeeper, saying 'Please care for this man. When I return, I'll pay you whatever it costs.'

"Which of the three travelers was a good neighbor?" asked Jesus.

Mary and Martha

Luke 10

Jesus had friends named Mary and Martha who were sisters. One day, Jesus stopped at Martha's home to visit. Mary was also there. The two sisters were happy to see Jesus. Martha went right to work fixing food and cleaning. She wanted everything perfect for Jesus!

While Martha worked, Mary sat at Jesus' feet, listening to him. His words were like cool, pure water to Mary. She gladly drank them in, not wanting to miss a single thing he said.

When Martha noticed how Mary was sitting with Jesus instead of helping, she became angry. "Lord," exclaimed Martha, "see how Mary just sits while I do all the work? You should tell her to help me."

"Martha, Martha," said Jesus calmly. "You are bothered by so many little things. Do you know what is really necessary?" Martha looked at Jesus with a puzzled face. "Mary made the right choice," said Jesus. "And it won't be taken from her."

THE BIG PARTY

Luke 14

"A very important man decided to throw a big party," said Jesus. "So he invited many friends. When everything was ready, he sent his servant out to tell his friends it was time to come. But all his friends made excuses. When the servant returned and told the man that no one was coming, the man felt very sad.

"The man said to his servant, 'Go out to the streets and back alleys. I want you to look for poor people, blind people, people who are lame or crippled. Invite them all to my party!' The servant did as his master said, but there was still room for more guests. 'Go again,' said the master. 'This time invite everyone who wasn't invited earlier. My house will be full of my new friends!'"

A LOST LAMB

Matthew 18

"Think about this," said Jesus: "A man owns a hundred sheep. Every evening, he counts to see that his sheep have come in safely from the hills. But one night, he discovers a little lamb has become lost. Do you think that just because this shepherd still has ninety-nine sheep, he will forget about the one that is missing? No, he goes out into the night, and he searches for his lost lamb.

"The shepherd is overjoyed when he finds his little lamb. He's not thinking about the ninety-nine who are safe and sound. No, he rejoices over this little one that was in danger. And the shepherd carries that lamb upon his shoulders and takes it back to safety. The reason I tell you this story," explained Jesus, "is so you will understand how much your Father in heaven cares about you. He is like that shepherd, and he does not want one single one to be lost!"

THE BLIND MAN

Mark 10

A crowd followed as Jesus approached Jericho. At the edge of town sat a poor blind man named Bartimaeus. When he heard that Jesus was passing by, he began to yell with all his might. "Jesus!" he cried. "Son of David, have mercy on me!" People nearby tried to quiet Bartimaeus. But the more they tried, the louder he shouted. "Son of David!" he hollered. "Please, have mercy on me!"

Jesus stopped walking and turned to his disciples. "Call that man to me," he said.

The disciples went to Bartimaeus. "Cheer up!" they said. "Get on your feet and come with us. Jesus is calling for you." Tossing down his cloak, the blind man went with them.

"What do you want me to do?" asked Jesus.

"Teacher," said Bartimaeus, "I wish to see."

"Go," said Jesus. "Because of your faith, you are healed." Instantly, Bartimaeus could see. He followed Jesus, looking at everything as he went!

ZACCHAEUS
THE TAX COLLECTOR

Luke 19

Zacchaeus was a tax collector. When Zacchaeus heard Jesus was in town, he wanted to see him. But Zacchaeus was short, and Jesus was always surrounded by a crowd. So Zacchaeus decided to climb a sycamore tree. From there he could watch for Jesus. He watched as Jesus stopped right beneath his tree. Jesus looked straight up at him.

"Zacchaeus," said Jesus with a smile. "Come on down. I want to stay at your house today."

Zacchaeus hopped down. "You are welcome at my house, Jesus," said the little man.

But others grumbled. "Why does Jesus want to go home with a sinner?"

Zacchaeus turned to Jesus and said, "Look, Lord. I promise to give half of my money to the poor. If I have cheated anyone in taxes, I will pay them back four times that amount."

"Salvation comes to Zacchaeus's house today," announced Jesus. "I have come to look for and save those who are lost."

A WIDOW'S GIFT

Luke 20–21

Jesus warned his disciples, "Watch out for those who teach the law. They like parading in fancy clothes and being seen in the marketplace. They always want the best. And yet they often treat poor widows unfairly. Men like that will be punished one day."

Jesus looked up and saw a rich man proudly place money into the temple treasury. Then a poor widow quietly dropped two small coins into the box. "The truth is that poor widow gave more than all the others. The others gave out of many riches, but she gave all the money she has in the world."

160

THE GOOD SHEPHERD

John 10

One day Jesus said, "If a man sneaks over the fence to get into a sheep pen, he probably is a thief. If he calls the sheep, they won't come because he's a stranger. His voice frightens them and they run away. But the real shepherd enters though the gate. And when he calls his sheep, he uses their names, and they know his voice.

"I am the good shepherd. I know each of my sheep by name, and my sheep know me.

"Sometimes a man is hired to watch over the sheep," continued Jesus. "But this man does not really care about them. He just works to get paid. If a wolf comes in the middle of the night, the man runs away. The wolf attacks the sheep and scatters the flock. The man doesn't even care because they're not his sheep.

"But I am the good shepherd," said Jesus. "And I lay down my life for my sheep.

"My Father loves me, and I gladly lay down my life for my sheep. Even though he has told me to do this, I do it because I want to. No man will take my life from me. Instead, I give it freely."

Lazarus, Wake Up!

John 11

Jesus received a message from Mary and Martha, saying their brother was sick.

After two days, Jesus said he would go to Lazarus.

Martha met Jesus at the edge of town. "Lord," she cried, "if you had been here sooner, my brother would be alive. Still, I know God will give you what you ask."

"Lazarus will come back to life," said Jesus.

"I know he will come to life in the resurrection at the last day," said Martha.

"I am the resurrection and the life," said Jesus. "Anyone who believes in me will live even if he dies. Do you believe in this, Martha?"

"Yes, Lord," she answered.

Martha went home to tell Mary that Jesus had come. Then Mary hurried to the edge of town too. "Lord," sobbed Mary, "if you had been here, my brother would not have died!"

"Where have you laid Lazarus?" Jesus asked.

As they walked, Jesus cried too.

"Remove the stone," Jesus commanded, his face wet with tears.

"But Lord," said Martha, "Lazarus has been dead for days."

"Believe and see God's glory," said Jesus.

In a loud voice he called, "Lazarus, come out!"

Out stepped a man wrapped in cloth! "Help him remove the grave clothes so he can walk," said Jesus.

Mary's Gift

John 12

Martha served a special dinner to honor Jesus. Her brother Lazarus was also there. After a while, Mary came in. She opened up a jar of sweet-smelling perfume. It was rare and quite valuable. To everyone's surprise, Mary poured out this rare perfume right onto Jesus' feet. And she used her own hair to wipe his feet. This was her way to show how much she loved Jesus.

"Mary, what have you done?" cried Judas Iscariot. "You've wasted all that costly perfume! It should have been sold and the money given to the poor." But Judas was thinking only of himself. When no one was looking, he often stole from the disciples.

"Mary has done what is right and good," said Jesus gently. "This perfume is to be my burial ointment. You see, I will not be with you much longer. But you will always be able to give to the poor."

ENTERING JERUSALEM

Mark 11

Jesus came to a small village near Jerusalem. He told two of his disciples, "Go into the town and near the entrance you will find a colt that has never been ridden. Untie the colt and bring it back. If anyone asks you what you are doing, tell them that the Lord needs the colt, and he will return it later."

The two did as Jesus said and soon returned with the colt. Then Jesus sat on the colt and began to ride.

As Jesus entered Jerusalem, people put their coats and garments across the road. Others spread palm branches they had cut from the nearby trees. A joyful parade followed Jesus as he rode the young colt through Jerusalem. The celebration continued as the crowd waved and shouted praises.

"Hosanna! Hosanna!" they cried. "Blessed is he who comes in the name of the Lord! Hosanna in the highest!"

THE SERVANT OF ALL

John 13

Right before Passover, Jesus shared a special meal with his disciples. He wanted to show his disciples how much he loved them. Before the meal, Jesus wrapped a towel around his waist and poured water into a bowl. Then he knelt before Simon Peter.

"No!" said Peter. "You can't wash my feet."

"If I don't, you are not part of me," explained Jesus.

"Oh," said Peter. "Then wash all of me!"

"Only your feet need be washed," said Jesus as he continued washing. "You see, a person who has already bathed is clean, but his feet get dirty when he walks along the road." After Jesus washed all the disciples' feet, he sat back down.

"Do you know why I did that?" he asked. "You call me Lord, and that is right. But today I gave you something to remember. See how I served you? I want you to serve each other in the same way. And if you do these things, you will be blessed."

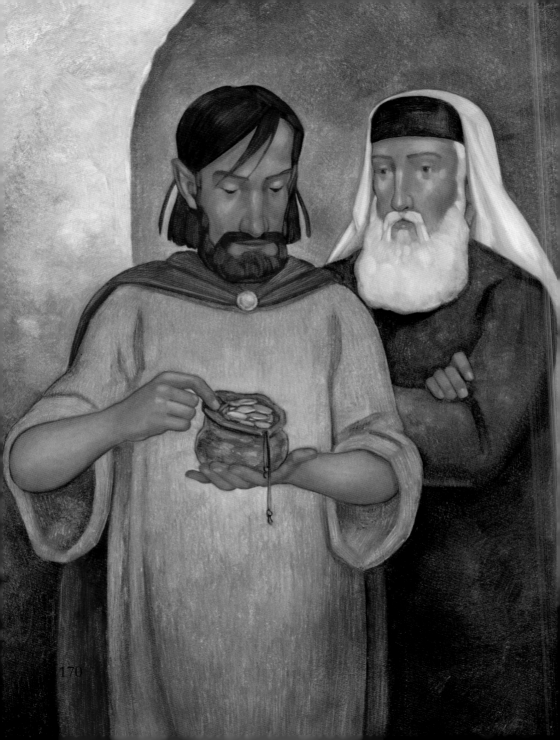

THE BETRAYER

Matthew 26

Judas Iscariot heard that the high priests wanted to get rid of Jesus. And Judas knew they had lots of money. So he went to the priests and asked, "What will you give me if I turn Jesus over to you?"

The high priests gave Judas thirty silver coins. And from then on, Judas looked for a chance to betray Jesus.

JESUS KNOWS

John 13

"It is meant to happen," Jesus explained. "Scripture says the one who eats bread with me will also betray me. I'm telling you now, so when it happens you will understand."

A disciple who dearly loved Jesus leaned over and asked, "Who is the betrayer, Lord?"

"I will dip this bread and give it to the one," said Jesus. Then he dipped the bread and handed it to Judas Iscariot.

When Judas took the bread from Jesus, Satan entered into him.

"Go quickly," said Jesus to Judas. "Do what you must do."

Judas Iscariot left Jesus and the other disciples.

THE LORD'S SUPPER

Matthew 26, John 13

Jesus continued to eat supper with the remaining eleven disciples. As they ate, Jesus held up a piece of bread. First he gave thanks for it, then he broke it into pieces and shared it with his disciples.

"Take and eat this," he said. "This is my body."

Then Jesus took a cup of wine and gave thanks. He shared it with his disciples saying, "Drink from this cup. This is my blood which will be poured out so that many can receive forgiveness for their sins.

"I will not drink any fruit of the vine until I drink it together with you, when we meet again in my Father's house."

"NOT ME, LORD"

John 13–14

"Love each other the way I have loved you," said Jesus. "When people see how much you love each other, they will know you are my disciples."

"But where are you going?" asked Simon Peter.

"You cannot go with me now," said Jesus.

"Why can't I follow you?" asked Peter. "I would lay down my life for you!"

"Peter," said Jesus, "before the rooster crows tomorrow morning, you will deny me three times."

MY FATHER'S HOUSE

John 14

"Don't be worried," said Jesus. "Trust God. He has a huge house with many rooms. And I am going to get your place ready. Then I'll come back for you."

"How will we get there?" asked Thomas.

"I am the way," said Jesus. "I am the truth and the life. No one comes to the Father except through me. If you see me, you see the Father. When I go to the Father, you can ask anything in my name, and I will do it to bring glory to the Father."

LIKE A VINE

John 15

"I am like a vine," said Jesus, "and you are like my branches. I want you to cling to me in the same way that a branch clings to a vine. My father is like the gardener who will prune and care for the vine. When the branches are healthy they bear good fruit. They are part of the vine. That's how I want you to be—a part of me.

"I love you the same way my Father loves me. Stay in my love. Let my love stay in you."

IN THE GARDEN

Matthew 26

That night, Jesus took his disciples to a quiet garden called Gethsemane. "Stay here and pray while I go over there," said Jesus. Then he turned to Peter, James, and John, and said, "My heart is breaking with sadness. Stay here to watch and pray."

Jesus went ahead of them. He cried out to the Father, "If it is possible, please remove this task from me. But don't do my will, Father; only let your will be done."

When Jesus returned to his disciples, he found they had all fallen asleep. So, in his darkest hour, Jesus prayed alone.

Finally, Jesus finished praying. He went back and woke up his disciples. "The time has come for the Son of Man to be betrayed," he said. "Look, here comes my betrayer now."

Arrested!

Luke 22, Mark 14

Men armed with swords and clubs marched to where Jesus and the disciples stood. The angry crowd was led by Judas, who had already set up a signal for the soldiers. He would kiss the man they were to arrest. When Judas kissed Jesus, Jesus asked, "Judas, do you betray the Son of Man with a kiss?"

Immediately the guards seized Jesus. Then Simon Peter grabbed a sword and cut off the ear of the high priest's servant.

"That is enough," said Jesus. Then he touched the servant and healed his ear. Jesus turned to the priests and temple guards. "Am I leading a rebellion that you come with weapons?"

Then they took Jesus to the home of the high priest to be questioned. The frightened disciples ran away.

PETER DENIES JESUS

Matthew 26, Luke 22

Peter was warming himself by a fire in the high priest's
courtyard when a servant girl asked, "Weren't you with Jesus?"

"I don't know him," said Peter. Later, someone else asked the
same thing and once again Peter denied knowing Jesus.

An hour later, another man spoke to Peter. "Surely you're one
of Jesus' followers. You even talk like him."

"I don't know what you're talking about!" cried Peter. Just
then a rooster crowed, and Peter remembered Jesus' words.
Moments later, as Jesus was being led by the guards, he turned
and looked at Peter. Peter went away and cried bitterly.

JESUS IS QUESTIONED

Luke 22

The guards beat Jesus. They covered his eyes with a blindfold and struck him. "If you're a prophet," they yelled, "tell us who is hitting you now!" Then they spat on him.

After that, Jesus was questioned. "Tell us if you are the Christ," demanded the high priest.

"If I say so," said Jesus, "you will not believe me. And if I ask, you will not answer. But from now on, the Son of Man will sit at the right hand of God."

"So," they said, "are you the Son of God?"

"You are right," said Jesus. "I am."

"There!" they said. "We've heard enough!"

PILATE AND HEROD

Luke 23

The priests and elders bound Jesus with ropes and dragged him before the Roman governor, Pilate.

"So are you the King of the Jews?" Pilate asked.

"Yes," said Jesus. "It is as you say."

Pilate asked a few more questions, then turned to the people and said, "I see no reason to punish this man." But the priests and elders didn't like that answer. So Pilate sent Jesus to stand before Herod.

Herod asked Jesus lots of questions, hoping that Jesus would perform a miracle. But Jesus remained silent. So Herod and his soldiers mocked Jesus then sent him back to Pilate.

"I still see no reason to kill this man," said Pilate to the Jewish leaders. But they would not listen. They demanded that Jesus be killed.

"But why?" cried Pilate. "For what crime?"

"Crucify him!" cried the angry crowd. "Crucify him!"

THE CROSS

Luke 23

Soldiers placed a crown of thorns on Jesus' head, then mocked him, saying, "Hail, King of the Jews!" Then they led Jesus to the place of death called The Skull. They nailed his hands and feet to a rough wooden cross. Two criminals also hung on crosses, one on each side of Jesus.

From the cross, Jesus looked down on the people and said, "Forgive them, Father, for they don't know what they are doing."

Some of the people made fun of Jesus, "You saved others; now see if you can save yourself!" Even the man on a cross next to Jesus joined in the mocking.

But the man on the other cross stopped him. "You are about to die! Don't you fear God at all? We did horrible things. We deserve to die. But Jesus is innocent." He turned to Jesus. "Please, Jesus, remember me when you come into your kingdom."

"This day, you will join me in paradise," Jesus answered.

THE DARKEST HOUR

Luke 23

Then, although it was still the middle of the day, darkness swallowed the sunlight. The air became still.

"Father!" cried Jesus. "Into your hands I commit my spirit!" Then Jesus breathed his last breath. And in that black and lonely moment, Jesus died.

The earth grew deathly silent, and the sky remained hopelessly dark. And down in Jerusalem, the great curtain in the temple was ripped from top to bottom!

"Surely this was a righteous man," said a centurion. Those who loved Jesus stood off in the distance crying.

HE LIVES!

Matthew 27–28, John 20

A large stone was placed in front of the opening to Jesus' tomb. The Pharisees asked Pilate to place guards at the tomb to make sure that no one would steal Jesus' body.

After the Sabbath, Mary Magdalene went to the tomb early in the morning. When she reached the tomb, she found the stone was rolled away. She turned and ran back down the road until she came to Peter and John.

"They have taken our Lord out of the tomb!" she cried. "I don't know where they have put him!"

The disciples ran on to the tomb too. They didn't know what to think. So the disciples returned to their homes.

Mary remained at the tomb, crying. But when she looked up, she saw two angels.

"Why are you crying, Mary?" asked the angels.

"They took my Lord. I don't know where they have put him." Then Mary saw a man. She thought he was the gardener. "Sir," she asked, "if you have taken him away, please tell me."

"Mary," he said. And instantly, Mary realized it was Jesus standing right in front of her.

"Teacher!" she cried.

"Do not touch me," said Jesus, "for I haven't been to the Father yet. But go and tell the others." So Mary ran and told the others that Jesus had risen from the dead!

197

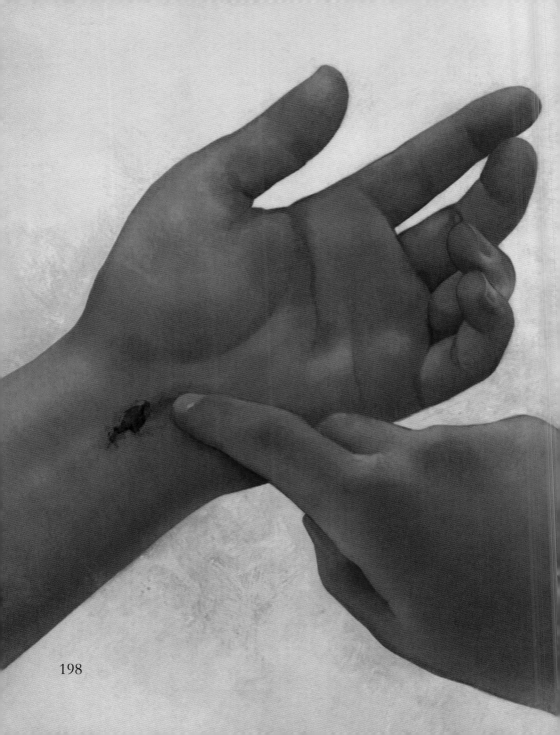

Thomas Has Doubts

John 20

During the next few days, many of the disciples saw Jesus. But Thomas did not see him. And so Thomas had a hard time believing that Jesus had really risen from the dead. Thomas told the others, "Unless I see the holes in his hands where the nails went through, I won't believe that Jesus is alive."

A week later, Jesus appeared to the disciples again. This time Thomas was there. "Touch the holes in my hands," said Jesus as he showed Thomas the nail holes. "Now stop doubting and believe."

"You are my Lord and God," said Thomas.

200

A BIG CATCH OF FISH

John 21

One morning, some of the disciples decided to go fishing.
They fished all night without catching a thing.

Someone called from the shore, "Catching any fish?"

"None," they called back.

"Try tossing your net on the right side of the boat," called
the stranger. And when they did, the net became so full of fish
they could hardly drag it back into the boat.

"It's Jesus!" shouted John. Then Peter dove into the sea and
swam to shore. The others followed in the boat. When they all
gathered on the shore, Jesus shared breakfast with them.

PETER'S SECOND CHANCE

John 21

Jesus turned to Peter and said, "Peter, do you love me?"

"Yes," said Peter. "You know I love you."

"Then feed my lambs," said Jesus. Again he asked Peter, "Do you really love me?"

"Yes, Lord," said Peter. "You know that I love you."

"Then take care of my sheep," said Jesus. And for a third time, Jesus asked him, "Peter, do you love me?"

Peter felt bad because Jesus had asked him this question three times. Peter cried out, "Lord, you know everything; surely you must know that I love you."

"Then feed my sheep," said Jesus.

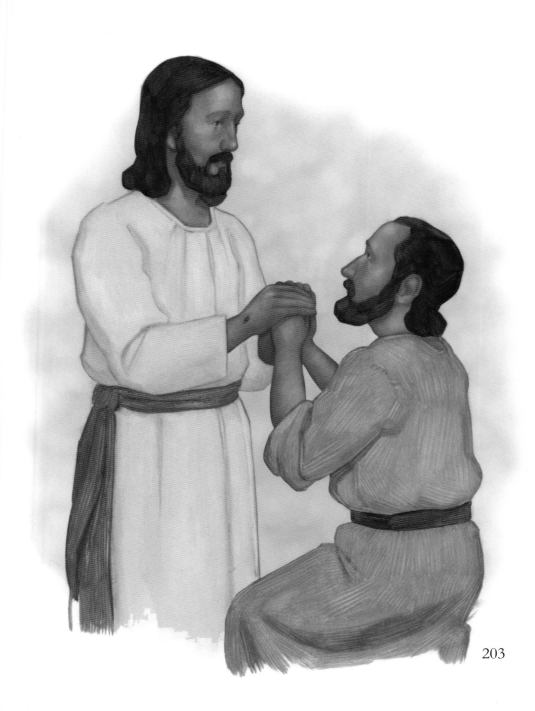

A JOB TO DO

Matthew 28, Mark 16

Jesus told his disciples to meet him on a mountain, and there he gave them a special job to do.

"Go into the world," said Jesus, "and tell everyone the good news. Teach others how to be my disciples. Show them how to do the things I have taught you. And baptize them in the name of the Father and the Son and the Holy Spirit.

"And remember this: I will always be with you, even to the very end of time."

JESUS SENDS A HELPER

Acts 2

Many days later, the disciples were gathered in one place. Suddenly a sound like a loud, roaring wind whipped through the room. The disciples stared in wonder as a small flame came to rest on each one of them. In that same moment, they were all filled with the Holy Spirit. The power they received from the Holy Spirit made them able to speak in languages they had never known before.

The disciples went out into the streets, speaking their new languages. When visitors heard the disciples talking about God in their own languages, they were completely amazed.

Peter spoke to the huge crowds. He told about how Jesus had died and come back to life, and how they too could be saved.

And 3,000 people listened to this message and were baptized that very day!

RISE UP AND WALK

Acts 3

One day, Peter and John went to the temple to pray. When they reached the gates, they saw a man who couldn't walk. Each day this man's friends would set him by the temple gates to beg for money.

"Please," begged the man. "Can you help the poor?"
Peter and John both stopped.

"Look at us," said Peter. "I do not have any silver or gold. But I do have this." Then Peter bent down, took the man's hand, and said, "In the name of Jesus Christ, I say to you, rise up and walk!"

The man leaped to his feet in joy! And he went with them to the temple, walking and jumping and praising God all the way. Everyone who had known this man stared in wonder.

SAUL SEES THE LIGHT

Acts 9

A man named Saul hated the followers of Jesus. One day, as Saul traveled to Damascus, a bright light from heaven flashed down upon him and he fell to the ground.

"Saul! Saul!" said a voice. "Why do you hate me?"

"Who are you?" asked Saul.

"I am Jesus," replied the voice. "Now get up and go to the city. You'll be told what you must do." But when Saul got up, he could not see. He was led to Damascus. And for three days Saul did not eat or drink. He only prayed.

Finally, God sent Ananias to visit Saul. Ananias put his hands on Saul and prayed. Instantly, Saul was able to see again. He was baptized, and then spent time learning about Jesus from the disciples. Soon Saul was telling everyone about Jesus—the same man he used to hate. Saul was a brand-new man, and he began to go by a new name. He became known as Paul.

PAUL'S SHIPWRECK ADVENTURE

Acts 27–28

Paul became a mighty preacher for Jesus. But when he went to Jerusalem, the Jews made trouble for him. He was beaten and arrested. But that didn't stop Paul.

Finally, Paul was put on a ship with other prisoners. When a horrible storm came up, God showed Paul that the ship would be wrecked, but everyone who stayed on board would make it safely to an island. Paul told the others about this.

It happened just as Paul said. The ship was wrecked, but they all made it to the island of Malta. On the island, Paul gathered some wood for a fire, but a deadly snake jumped out and bit him. The islanders said, "The prisoner must be very bad. Now he will get what he deserves." But Paul didn't even get sick.

God used Paul's shipwreck to bring the good news to the island of Malta. And when Paul was put back in prison, God helped him write letters to encourage others.

THE HOLY CITY

Revelation 21

Another one of Jesus' disciples spent some time on an island, too. While John was there, God showed him what it will be like when Jesus takes his believers home to heaven.

There will be a new heaven and a new earth. All sadness, crying, sickness, and death will be gone. The new city of God will be enormous and beautiful. A spectacular wall will surround the city like a glittering rainbow made of millions of colorful jewels. And there will be twelve giant gates in the wall, each made of solid pearl. The streets will be polished gold that glistens like glass. And the buildings will be a shimmering gold and glass.

JESUS IS COMING BACK

Revelation 22

At the end there will be no need for a temple, for the Father and Son will be there. There will be no need for sun or moon, for God's glory will be brighter than the summer sun.

A crystal-clear river of life will flow from the throne of God and through the city. The tree of life will grow there, bringing forth new fruit. And the leaves of this tree will heal all the nations.

Jesus said, "Behold, I am coming soon! I am the First and the Last, the Beginning and the End. Yes, I am coming soon."

Amen. Come, Lord Jesus.

Let's Go Explore Series

Kim Washburn

In these full-color picture books, young readers travel to the holy lands. Complete with photographs, maps, vocabulary call-outs, fun facts, and more, this is the perfect resource for the young explorer. Read about the Biblical significance and history as well as current and curious information about foods, clothes, places of interest, and other pertinent facts.

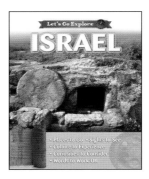

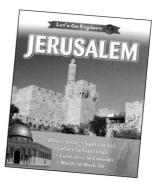

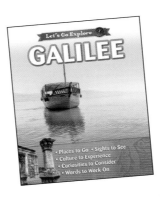

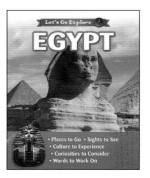

Available in stores and online!

ZONDER**kidz**™
.com

1001 Bible Questions Kids Ask

The Bible is God's Word to his people, so it has some important things to say! But let's be honest...it can also be sort of puzzling.

Now you can get relief for your confused cranium.

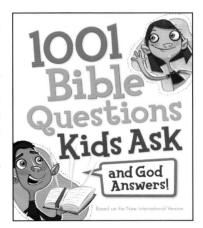

Here's how:

- Pick up this book, based on the NIV translation.
- Look up your questions.
- Learn about heaven, earth, angels, sin, creation, and more.
- Understand what the creator of the universe — your Creator — is saying to you!

Available in stores and online!

Adventure Bible for Early Readers, NIrV

Lawrence O. Richards

Ready for Adventure? *The Adventure Bible for Early Readers* takes you on a fun, exciting journey through God's Word. Along the way you'll meet all types of people, see all sorts of places, and learn all kinds of things about the Bible. Most importantly, you'll grow closer in your relationship with God. Here's a quick tour through the features:

- "Life in Bible Times" Articles and illustrations describe what life was like in ancient days
- "People in Bible Times" Offers close-up looks at amazing people of the Bible
- "Did You Know?" Provides interesting facts that help you better understand God's Word.
- "Let's Live It!" Includes hands-on activities to help you apply biblical truths to your life.
- "Words to Treasure" Highlights great verses to memorize.
- A Dictionary/concordance for those tricky words.
- Book Introductions for basic facts about each book of the Bible (who wrote it, where it took place, and why it was written).
- 20 color pages with games, a scavenger hunt, and other Bible fun, with a jungle safari theme.
- 8 pages of color maps.

Visit www.zondervan.com for a complete listing of all bindings available.

Available in stores and online!

NIrV Kids' Quest Study Bible

Real Questions,
Real Answers

How come people lived so long back then? Why did God allow the flood? Is Jesus real?

Kids have LOTS of questions about the Bible and God.

The *NIrV Kid's Quest Study Bible* is a great resource for kids eager to learn more.

- Over 500 real questions and answers from kids
- Quest Challenges help kids apply the Bible's teachings to their own lives by pointing to Scripture
- Book introductions help explain what each book of the Bible is about
- A dictionary and subject guide help kids find what they're looking for
- Fresh, colorful design with cartoons makes the Bible fun to look at and use
- The complete NIrV translation — the NIV for kids!

Visit www.zondervan.com for a complete listing of all bindings available.

Available in stores and online!

NIrV Kids Study Bible, Revised

The *NIrV Kids' Study Bible* starts early readers off right reading and studying God's Word. With its vivid, full-color pictures and simple language, the bestselling *NIrV Kids' Study Bible* is the perfect way to get early readers digging into God's Word for the first time. This Bible uses the complete text of the New International Reader's Version® written at a third grade reading level.

Features include:

- Check It Out: sketches and descriptions of what life was like in Bible times
- Brain Game: questions to help kids remember important Bible themes
- Soak It up: key verses highlighted for kids to memorize
- Book Introductions: brief overviews of each book with an outline of key events
- Full-color pages illustrated by artist Joel Tanis bring Bible characters and events to life
- Single-column format for easy reading

Available in stores and online!